Happy Birthday,
Strawberry Shortcake!

GROSSET & DUNLAP
Penguin Young Readers Group
An Imprint of Penguin Random House LLC

ISBN 978-0-448-48748-9   10 9 8 7 6 5 4 3 2 1

Happy Birthday,
Strawberry Shortcake!

By Mickie Matheis
Illustrated by Laura Thomas

Grosset & Dunlap
An Imprint of Penguin Random House

It was a beautiful day in Berry Bitty City, and
Strawberry Shortcake had been busy baking all
morning. She needed more flour to make one last
treat—a cream-filled, berry-topped cake. She walked
from her café over to the Orange Mart to get a bag.

When she opened the door of Orange Blossom's store, Strawberry
heard excited chatter. All her friends were standing inside.
"Hi, girls!" she said cheerfully.

Strawberry's friends immediately stopped talking and began
to act strangely. Orange Blossom crumpled up a piece of paper
and threw it over her shoulder. Blueberry Muffin started to dig
frantically through her purse.

Plum Pudding, who had been doing a pirouette,
stopped in mid-twirl and sat down on a box.

Cherry Jam noisily dropped a clipboard into a wastebasket and turned to study a shelf of canned vegetables.

Raspberry Torte stepped in front of Lemon Meringue,
who held a shopping basket. "Uh . . . Ha-ha . . . Hi there,
Strawberry!" Raspberry stammered with a wave of her hand.

Orange rushed over to Strawberry. "What can I help you with, Strawberry?" she asked nervously.

"I just need a bag of flour," answered the little redhead, looking around at her friends.

"Here you go!" Orange said, shoving a bag into Strawberry's hands and hurrying her out the door. "Thanks for coming by!"

"*Whew! That was close!*"
Orange said to the others
after Strawberry had left.

The girls had been planning a
surprise party for Strawberry's
birthday the next day. They hoped that
their friend didn't suspect anything.

"Okay, does everyone know what to do?"
Lemon asked.

"Yes!" Plum exclaimed, spinning around the
store. "I'm so excited!"

"See you tomorrow at my place," said
Blueberry with a big smile.

"This is going to be the berry best party ever!"

Raspberry said enthusiastically.

And it would have been—except nothing went according to plan!

Lemon forgot to set the timer on her oven and burned the birthday cake she was making for Strawberry.

Orange discovered that her party supplies were all sold out.

Raspberry accidentally broke the pretty pink dessert tray that the girls had gotten as a gift for Strawberry.

Plum couldn't find her favorite pair of dance shoes, and the strings on Cherry's guitar snapped, so they couldn't perform the birthday song-and-dance number they had planned.

Blueberry knocked glitter all over the glue-covered
card she was making for Strawberry.
The card was ruined.

"This is going to be the berry worst party ever!"

she cried.

Later that day, the girls met at Blueberry's bookstore to discuss all their party-planning disasters. Everything was such a mess—what else could possibly go wrong?

Just then, the phone rang. It was Huckleberry Pie calling from Berry Big City.

"Blueberry, I'm sorry, but my pet-mobile isn't running. I'm not going to make it to Strawberry's party," said Huck.

Blueberry put her head in her hands. "This is terrible." She sniffled. "Now we can't have a party for Strawberry on her berry big day!"

Suddenly the door of the bookstore flew open. Pupcake and Custard rushed in carrying a bunch of red balloons.

"What's this?"
Lemon asked, reaching for them.

Each balloon had a girl's name on it and
a note inside. "I can't read it," said Cherry,
staring into her balloon.

"Then let's pop them!" Orange suggested. "One . . . two . . . three!"
The girls jumped on their balloons, and—

Pop!

—the papers that were hidden inside fluttered to the floor.
"Please come to the Berry Café right away," the notes read.

Please Come to the Berry Café right away!

The girls exchanged puzzled looks.

What is Strawberry up to?

They all headed across town to the Berry Café. As they were about to walk inside, a voice from above called out, "Hello there!"

The girls looked up to see Huck floating down on a butterfly. "This butterfly just showed up at my house with a note saying to jump on and fly here!" he explained, hopping off and waving good-bye to the butterfly.

This is so strange, Blueberry said to herself as she reached for the doorknob of the café. *What is going on?*

When Blueberry saw what was inside, she was even more surprised! The café was decorated with pink, green, and yellow balloons and streamers.

Lunch was served at a table set for eight. In the center of the table sat a berry beautiful cake.

Just then Strawberry jumped up from behind the counter.
"Surprise!" she called out to her friends.
    But everyone was still confused. "What's this?" they asked.
"A birthday celebration!" Strawberry replied.

"But we were supposed to throw a party for you," Orange pointed out.

"No," Strawberry corrected her. "You're supposed to make my birthday happy. And guess what? You already do that—just by being my berry best friends. So I wanted to do something on my birthday to show you how much I appreciate all of you!"

The girls and Huck gathered around Strawberry and gave her a big hug. "Strawberry, you make every day happy for us—just by being you." Lemon smiled and gave her friend a big squeeze.

"Happy birthday,
Strawberry Shortcake!"